PAPA ANANSI

& His Spectacular Spider Stories

Georgina Simmons

JOBA Ltd

JP

To my forever baby brother
"Let brotherly love continue…"
-Hebrews 13:1

" I am not African because I was born in Africa, but because Africa was born in me...."

KWAME NKRUMAH

CONTENTS

PROLOGUE

Hi everyone, Jozzie here.

The first time I met Papa Anansi, he revealed something very important to me, something not even my mum had told me.

Pay attention, because between the pages of this book, I know he is going to reveal something very special about you too.....

xxx

Jozzie Taylor

#thechroniclesofjozzietaylor
#whichclanareyoureppin

THE STORY BEGINS...

ONE

GREETINGS FROM
PAPA ANANSI

My dear friend, how wonderful to meet you! Although I think I know why you are here....you have been seeing things you cannot explain, am I correct? Like the grumpy woman next door who hides her tail beneath her coat? Or the swimming instructor at the pool, who can hold her breath for an hour? Or perhaps it is your math teacher and his unexplainably long neck, or the librarian at the library who hisses when she speaks? All these curious curiosities have you scratching your head I bet! Well my friend, you are in luck! The answers to your ponderings and your wonderings are all right here.

Now, I know when you went to the bookshop today, you did not expect to choose this book. But what would you say if I told you, that *you* did not choose this book, this book chose YOU!

Are you surprised? You should not be, it is as clear as the trunk on an Elephantidae's face. You see my friend, you are incredibly special. You are sooooo special, you can do what no other human boy or girl, or any other human man or woman can. You can see Humanalia!

What are Humanalia, I hear you ask? Well, we are humans that can transform into animals. Yes, you heard me right 'we'. I am also one of them, actually I may be THE most famous Humanalia in the world.

I have eight black spindly legs and eight black eyes. I can scuttle up a tree faster than you can blink, and spin webs as strong as the whiskers on a walrus' face. Can you guess what I am? Correct again! I am an Arachnida but you probably know that by its most common name, spider. I am Papa Anansi, the spider-man.

There are thousands of us around you know. All of us like your neighbour and your teacher, and the swimming instructor and the librarian, but most humans cannot see us when we shift into our animal forms. Only we can see each other and of course now my clever pal, so can you.

I have lots and lots of stories to tell, about the world we come from and what we do. I have been waiting a *long, long* time for someone to tell them to and now I have you! But first, I need you to join me. Where you ask? Why here in the Kingdom of Cush of course. You do not need a car or a plane, or a boat or a train, all you need to do is press your nose once and blink three times.... and presto!

Here you are! Isn't this marvellous! What? Yes that is a turtle in trousers over there, and sitting by that gurgling stream is a gorilla playing a banjo. But come, let us not shilly-shally nor dilly-dally, there is much more in this magical Kingdom to see! Like mermaids and werewolves, and centaurs wearing shoes. There are witches and spell books, and talking cats in buttoned up waistcoats.

Right, phewww! Here we are, that was quite a walk, but I am sure you would agree it was worth it. You see this wonderful tree, the one with the fruit that dazzle like a thousand gems? Well, buried at its bottom is a calabash, a beautiful wooden pot shaped like a drum. Now when you lift its lid, something marvellous is going to happen. Do you know what that is? No? I am going to tell you. All the stories ever told about Humanalia are going to come flying out and zip across the world like millions of excited bees! You do not believe me? Ok, come and sit right here, sit beside me in the shade of this tree and hold the calabash in your hand. Can you feel that? It is like holding electricity between your fingers. But wait! Before you peek inside, I want to tell you how I captured these tales in the first place.

You see, they did not always live here on earth. Oh no! Many many years ago, before the oldest person you know was born, the greatest stories ever told were captured and locked away. But I came up with a clever plan to free them! So now are you ready? Are you listening very carefully? Because our story begins way up there, within the blue blue cotton clouds of this beautiful sun lit sky....

TWO

HOW STORIES CAME
TO EARTH

A long time ago, in the Kingdom of Cush, there lived an Arachnida called Papa Anansi. He wandered over the Kingdom and over the earth, travelling on his web strings. Sometimes he looked like an old man and other times he looked like a spider.

In that long ago, there were no stories on Earth. The sky-god Nyame kept them all to himself. He locked them away in a beautiful golden box, never to be told or heard.

Papa Anansi wanted these stories. Just like his father and his father before him, and his father before him, Papa Anansi knew that they would tell the beginning and the ending of the world. But anyone who had ever tried to get them, always returned empty-handed.

One day Anansi decided to climb up his web to visit Nyame and ask him for his stories. When the powerful sky-god saw the thin, spidery old man scuttling up to his mighty throne, he opened his mouth and laughed a laugh that thundered over the earth. Nyame asked, "what makes you think that you, a mere Arachnida, can pay the price I ask for my stories?"

Papa Anansi asked him, "what is the price of your stories?"

"Hmm," said Nyame, "the price is not gold, nor is it silver. It is not diamonds and nor is it coins, the price of MY stories is greater than all of these things combined."

"Whatever it is, I will bring it to you," replied Anansi.

"I want just four things: the first is *Onini,*

the snake-man that swallows men whole; the second is *Osebo,* the leopard-man with teeth like spears; I want *Mmoboro,* the hornets that swarm and sting; and *Mmoatia,* the fairy who is never seen. Bring them all to me, and I will give you my stories."

Bowing, Papa Anansi turned and slid back down his web. If he was going to capture the four creatures, he was going to need the help of somebody clever. "Mamere the sorceress! She will know what to do," and so Anansi hurried to her house to tell her his plan.

"Go and cut the branch from a palm tree and cut some vines as well. Take them to the stream where Onini the snake-man lives," said Mamere.

"I understand, say no more," replied Papa Anansi.

He went off to the swampy stream, carrying the branches and the vines and then began arguing loudly with himself. "This is

14

longer than *he* is! You lie! No, it is true, this branch is longer and *he* is shorter, much shorter."

On the bank of the stream, Onini was listening. "What are you muttering about Papa Anansi?" he hissed.

"Oh Onini! I did not see you there! It is Mamere, the sorceress. She is *such* a liar! She says that you are longer than this palm branch and I say that you are NOT!"

"SSsssss!" said Onini, "come and place the branch next to me and we will see that it is *you* who is the liar Anansi."

And so Papa Anansi put the palm branch next to the snake-man's body. He watched craftily as the large Reptilia stretched himself alongside it. In a dash, Papa Anansi bound Onini to the branch with his vine, winding it over and over until he came to his head. Then he said loudly, "fool! I will now take you to Nyame, the sky-god."

Papa Anansi spun a web around the snake and carried him back through the clouds to the sky-kingdom.

But when he saw Onini Nyame merely said, "there remains what still remains."

So Papa Anansi dropped back down to Earth to find the next creature, Osebo the leopard-man, with teeth like spears.

Mamere said to him, "go dig a large hole."

Papa Anansi replied, "I understand, say no more."

After following Osebo's tracks, Papa Anansi dug a very deep pit. He covered it with the branches of the trees and went back home. Early the next morning, he returned and found the leopard-man lying in the pit. "Osebo, is that you? What are you doing down there?"

"Anansi! Help me! I was taking a walk last night and suddenly I fell into this hole!"

"Ah, ah Osebo! You should not be prowling

around at night. I will help you, put your paw here and here, and I will pull you out."

Osebo put his paws on the sticks that Papa Anansi placed over the pit, and began to climb up.

In an instant, Papa Anansi hit him over the head with a wooden club - *pow!* Osebo fell down and Papa Anansi quickly tied him to the sticks with his web string. "Fool! I will now take you to the sky-god."

But when he saw Osebo, Nyame merely said, "there remains what still remains."

And so Papa Anansi went looking for Mmoboro, the hornets that swarmed and stung. He told this to Mamere and she said, "look for an empty gourd and fill it with water."

Papa Anansi replied, "I understand, say no more." He did just that and then went walking through the bush, until he saw a swarm of hornets playing in a tree. He poured some of the water and sprinkled it all over their nest and then cut a leaf from a nearby banana tree. He held the leaf up and used it to cover his head. Papa Anansi then poured the rest of the water from the gourd all over himself. Then, standing dripping in his clothes, he called out, "the rain has come, the rain has come! Silly hornets, do you not see me standing here with a leaf to cover my head? Fly inside my empty gourd so that the rain will not beat at your wings."

The Mmoboro flew into the gourd, saying, "H*uuuummmm*! Y*ɛda wo ase*, we thank you Anansi!"

Quickly, Anansi covered the mouth of the gourd and spun a thick web around it. "Fools," he said, "I will now take you to the sky-god."

But when he saw the Mmoboro, Nyame merely said, "there remains what still remains."

So Papa Anansi dropped back down to

earth, to get the final creature - Mmoatia, the fairy who is never seen.

He went to Mamere to ask her what to do.

"Carve a child's wooden doll and cover it with sticky sap from a tree."

"I understand, say no more," Papa Anansi replied and did just that. Then, walking through the forest, he found the Odum tree, where the fairies like to play. Papa Anansi made a delicious dish of pounded yam and put some in the doll's hand. He made a little more and put that in a brass basin at her feet. Then Papa Anansi hid in the bushes holding onto one end of a vine creeper, the other, he had cleverly tied around the doll's neck.

It wasn't long before Mmoatia came to play. She saw the doll with the pounded yam and asked if she could have some. Papa Anansi pulled on his vine creeper and made the doll's head nod, "yes".

Mmoatia dug into the delicious food,

gobbling it up until it was all gone. Feeling full and happy, she thanked the doll, "*medasse*," but the doll did not reply. The fairy became very angry. "Do you not have any manners! I said thank you!"

In the bushes Papa Anansi began to giggle, but did not pull the vine creeper.

Hearing his muffled chuckle Mmoatia thought the doll was laughing at *her*. "Ah! You are laughing at me abi? Ok, I will give you something to laugh about!" Furious, she drew back her hand and slapped the doll – *pah!*

Her hand got stuck.

She lifted her other hand and slapped the doll with that one too – *pah!*

This hand also got stuck.

The fairy kicked out with one foot and then the other, sticking both feet to the wooden doll. Finally she pushed her stomach into it, completely gluing herself to the carved figurine.

Papa Anansi came out from his hiding place. "Fool! I will now take you to the sky-god." He spun a web around the last of the four creatures and brought Mmoatia up to Nyame in the sky-kingdom.

Seeing this last catch, the sky-god called together all the ancestors. "My esteemed elders, I say to you today, that this tiny spider-man has done what nobody before him has ever been able to do. From now until forever, my sky-god stories belong to you, Papa Anansi and we shall call them the "Spider Stories."

And so dear reader, this is how stories came to Earth, all because of the great cunning of one tiny being, Papa "Kwaku" Anansi.

The day Anansi brought the golden box to his home, he invited Mamere to join him. Together, they read and learnt every one of the stories, so that they could tell them to others who would also pass them down to their descendants.

You can still see them today dear friend, in the corners of your ceiling or below your window ledge, the Arachnida who tell these beautiful tales. They quickly spin them into their silk webs and if you look very *very* closely, you may even see the smiling face of Papa Anansi and his now empty golden box.

THREE

WHY MOSQUITOS BUZZ IN PEOPLE'S EARS

(Inspired by West African folklore)

One morning, Madame Aedes the mosquito was passing by the lake when she saw Papa Anansi sitting admiring his reflection.

She said to him, "Papa Anansi, you will never believe what I saw yesterday!"

"Hmph! What did you see?" replied Papa Anansi.

Madame Aedes said, "I saw a farmer digging his farm and he pulled up yams that were as BIG as me!"

"Pah!" spat Papa Anansi, "what is a mosquito compared to a yam? You know something, I am growing tired of your constant lying Madame. Everyday you are troubling me with your stories. I tell you now, I prefer to be deaf than listen to such nonsense!" Then mumbling angrily to himself, the spider-man stuck two sticks in his ears and disappeared into the tall tall grass, *scatter, scatter, scatter!*

Papa Anansi was still muttering away when he passed by Mr Mamba.

Mr Mamba looked up and said, "Ah! Good morning Papa Anansi."

But Papa Anansi did not answer. Instead he rushed by the snake-man still scowling and grumbling, *scatter, scatter, scatter!*

"Why did he not return my greeting?" wondered Mr Mamba, "hmm, he must be very angry about something. I know him that tricky little trickster! He is plotting against me!" So looking for a place to hide, Mr Mamba spotted a rabbit hole and in he slid, *ssswissshhhh, ssswissshhhh, ssswissshhhh!*

When Benjamin Buttering the rabbit, saw Mr Mamba slithering into his burrow, he ran out through a hole in the back and hopped away.

Mrs Rook, the crow, saw the terrified Benjamin fleeing and flew up into the forest. She began to cry *"Ka-kaa, ka-kaa!"* as it was her job to sound the alarm when danger was present in the Kingdom.

Mr Otinba heard the cry and sure it was a menacing beast stalking its prey, he beat his chest and began to screech. Mr Otinba leapt through the trees, swinging from the vines to help warn the others. *"Hoohooo-hee-haha!"*

As he crashed through the tree-tops, Mr Otinba landed on a branch. The branch broke and fell onto Mother Owl's nest.

Mother Owl was not there as she was

out looking for food to feed her hungry owlets. But when the branch broke, it killed one of her babies. When she returned to her nest, Mother Owl's remaining baby birds began to cry.

"It was Mr Otinba! He killed our brother!" they wailed.

Mother Owl sat in her treetop and cried a heartbroken cry, *"Whoooo-whoooo!"*

Like all the other Humanalia in the Kingdom, Mother Owl also had a job. In fact, her's was probably the most important job of all. She was to wake the sun each morning so that the day could begin. But now one of her babies was gone and the time she was supposed to hoot for the sun, she could not do it. So the nights grew longer and the day could not come. The Kingdom of Cush fell into perpetual darkness.

Finally King Musa, the king of Cush, called all the clans together. Mother Owl, with her broken heart, did not come and so Mamere the sorceress was sent to get her.

When she arrived, King Musa asked her, "Mother Owl, why have you not called the sun? The night is dragging on and on! Everyone in the Kingdom is worried."

Mother Owl said, "Mr Otinba killed one of my babies. My heart is broken and because of this, I cannot sing for the sun."

King Musa said, "my Kingdom, did you hear this? It was Mr Otinba who killed the baby owlet and broke Mother Owl's heart. Now she cannot sing for the sun."

King Musa called Mr Otinba to him.

The monkey-man came and stood before the King.

"Mr Otinba, why did you kill one of Mother Owl's owlets?"

"King Musa, it was Mrs Rook's fault! She was calling and screeching and warning us of danger, so I went leaping through the trees to help. A branch broke beneath me, and fell on Mother Owl's nest."

"King Musa replied," so it was Mrs Rook, who alarmed Mr Otinba, who broke the branch that killed the owlet and now Mother Owl cannot sing for the sun."

The King called for Mrs Rook, who came flapping her powerful black wings.

She said, "King Musa, it is all Benjamin Buttering's fault. I saw him fleeing like a frightened bunny for his life, and assumed he was in great danger. So I raised the alarm as it is my job to do."

King Musa nodded. "So it is Benjamin who scared Mrs Rook, who raised the alarm, that startled Mr Otinba, who broke the branch that killed the owlet and now Mother Owl cannot sing for the sun."

Then King Musa called for Benjamin Buttering who stood shaking and stuttering in front of the King.

"Benjamin, why were you running so quickly in the daytime?"

"Oh dear-dear King Musa," Benjamin stammered, "it was Mr Mamba's fault. I-I was in my house minding my own business when he slid in and chased me out!"

"Ahhh! So it was Mr Mamba, who frightened Benjamin, who ran through the Kingdom and scared Mrs Rook, who raised the alarm, that startled Mr Otinba, who broke the branch that killed the owlet and now Mother Owl cannot sing for the sun."

King Musa called for Mr Mamba. The giant python came slithering forward, *ssswaassswaa, ssswaassswaa, ssswaassswaa!*

"King Musa, it was Papa Anansi's fault. I greeted him and he would not speak to me, so I thought he was plotting against me. I slid into Benjamin's burrow so I could hide."

"Ah-ha! Now we are getting to the bottom of the matter, this is all Papa Anansi's fault. He ignored Mr Mamba, who frightened Benjamin, who ran through the Kingdom and scared Mrs Rook, who raised the alarm, that startled Mr Otinba, who broke the branch that killed the owlet and now Mother Owl cannot sing for the sun."

Papa Anansi had no idea of all that had happened. He was still wandering around with two sticks poking out of his ears. When he was summoned before the King, all the other clans began to laugh.

King Musa pulled out the sticks and said, "Papa Anansi, what mischief have you been plotting against Mr Mamba?"

"Me your majesty?" the spider-man cried, "I have not plotted against Mr Mamba, he is my friend!"

"Then why did you not return my greeting this morning?" Mr Mamba grumbled.

"Ah! Is that it? I did not hear you, nor did I see you. Madame Aedes told me such a BIG lie,

I could not bear to listen to her anymore, so I stuck these sticks into my ears."

"Ha!ha!ha!" laughed King Musa, "so that is why you are walking around like that?"

"Yes," replied Papa Anansi. "It is the mosquito's fault."

"So it was Madame Aedes who annoyed Papa Anansi who ignored Mr Mamba, who frightened Benjamin, who ran through the Kingdom and scared Mrs Rook, who raised the alarm, that startled Mr Otinba, who broke the branch that killed the owlet and now Mother Owl cannot sing for the sun."

"Punish Madame Aedes! Punish the mosquito!" all the clans cried

When Mother Owl heard this, she was glad. She faced the east where the sun was waiting and began to hoot; *"Hooo, hoooooo!"*

The sun hearing her, began to rise up into the sky.

Madame Aedes who had been listening

from a distance, crept under a leaf to hide. She could not be found and so was never brought before the King.

However, because of this, the mosquito has a guilty conscience. Till this day, she buzzes around, whining in people's ears, "*zeeeeeeee*, is everyone still angry with me?"

When she does that, she gets an honest answer in the form of a slap *"pow!"*

FOUR

HOW WISDOM CAME TO THE WORLD

If there was one thing Papa Anansi knew, it was that he was not wise. He was clever and he was tricky, and he could outwit many of the creatures who lived in the Kingdom of Cush, but he knew that he did not have very much wisdom. This bothered the spider-man a lot, but he did not know what to do about it.

Then one bright sunny day, Papa Anansi had a very clever thought. "I know," he said to himself, "if I can get all of the wisdom in the Kingdom and put it in a calabash, then I will be very wise. In fact, I would be the wisest Humanalia of all!"

And so he set out to find a suitable calabash and began his journey to collect all the wisdom he could find.

Papa Anansi went from door to door asking everyone to give some of their wisdom. The different Humanalia clans chuckled. Poor Papa Anansi! If any creature needed some wisdom, it was definitely him, so each of them put a little bit in his calabash and wished him well on his search.

Very soon the spider-man's calabash was overflowing and he couldn't hold anymore. Papa Anansi needed to find a place to store it all.

"By now I *must* be the wisest person, not just in Cush, but in the whole world! But if I don't find a good hiding place for my wisdom, I might lose it." Papa Anansi looked around him. He spotted a tall oak tree. "Ah-ha!" he said to himself, "if I climb to the highest branches of that tree, I can hide my wisdom in its branches and never have to worry about someone stealing it!"

Papa Anansi set out to climb the tree. First, he took a cloth band and tied it around his waist. Then he tied the calabash to the front of his stomach where it would be safe.

However, as he began to climb, the calabash kept getting in the way. He squirmed and squiggled and he turned and he wiggled, but he could not climb the way he needed to reach the top of the tree.

Just then Mr Dudu walked by. He peered up at the spider-man through the thick lenses of his glasses. "What are you doing Papa Anansi?" he asked.

"I am climbing this tree with my calabash full of wisdom," Anansi replied.

"But would it not be easier if you tied the calabash behind you instead of to your stomach?"

Papa Anansi glared down at the mole-man. "Shouldn't you be going home now?" he snapped. Mr Dudu chuckled and continued with his journey. When he was just a little speck in the distance, Papa Anansi moved the calabash behind him and continued up the tree with no problem.

When he reached the top, he cried, "I walked everywhere and searched all over Cush. I collected so much wisdom, that I am the wisest person in the world, but still Mr Dudu is wiser than me. All of you, take back your wisdom!" Furious, Papa Anansi lifted the calabash over his head and threw its contents into the wind. All the wisdom blew far and wide and settled over the land. And this is how wisdom came to the world.

FIVE

THE FIRST SIMPLES

(Inspired by Aboriginal folklore)

A long long time ago, in the Kingdom of Cush, in the Feral Lands of the Equidae clan, there was a time called Dream Time. This was when the Spirit of the Wilderness initiated the different humans into their Humanalia clans.

All the humans loved Dream Time. It was then that the totems they had been given at birth, would break and unite their soul with the soul of their spirit animal. This was a time of great celebration, with lots of singing and laughing and dancing.

When the day of Dream Time came, the

Spirit of the Wilderness called all the leaders of the different clans. "Bring your people," it said.

And so first came the Equidae, those connected to horses. Their leader was a great warrior called Kokou. He had a powerful bow that could defeat any enemy in battle.

The Aves came next, those connected to birds. Their leader was called Maat, she had a feather that could tell if there was goodness in a creature's heart.

Then came the Ursidae, those connected to bears. Their leader was called Navajo and he wielded a magical spear.

Finally there came the Canidae, those who were connected to wolves. Their leader was called Funris. He did not have a magical object but he was fearsome and he was strong.

When the clans came together, they were very happy to see each other. They sang and danced and whispered amongst themselves, *"what animal do you think I will be?"* because although they were born into a particular clan, sometimes the Spirit of the Wilderness would see they were not suited to it and change their spirit animal.

As they sang and they danced, there was a great rushing sound like a storm blowing over a house. It was The Spirt of the Wilderness, it had come to dwell amongst them!

All the Equidae and the Ave and even the Ursidae, dropped to their knees as a sign of respect. Only the Canidae continued to stand on their feet, staring boldly around them.

As the Spirit settled, it began to speak to them all. "I am going to show you what you must teach your sons before they become Humanalia, and what you must teach your daughters before they become Humanalia too. But first I need you to clear this area and make a big space for the ceremony."

The clans did as instructed. The Equidae cleared away the bushes and the grass, and the Ave picked up all the stones. The Ursidae carried away the branches and when it was time to move the heavy logs, the Equidae pitched in to help them. Everyone was doing what they had been told to do, all except the Canidae.

They continued to dance around, and sing their songs, and clap their hands and eat. The Spirit of the Wilderness saw this, but it did not say a thing. It was well known throughout Cush that although the Canidae were strong, they were lazy and stubborn and did not like being told what to do.

The Canidae watched the other clans clearing and making a space for the ceremony and they sat back and howled with laughter.

Kokou grabbed his bow, and in anger aimed it at Funris' heart. But Navajo quickly intervened and held him back.

"Pay them no mind," the wise Ursidae said, "nothing good has ever come from being idle."

In her hand Maat's feather began to glow. "See," she said showing it to Navajo, "their laziness is taking over the goodness that dwells inside them."

The Canidae overheard what was being said about them and began to make fun of the other clans. By now the Spirit of the Wilderness was very angry.

It moved like a great storm to where the Canidae were gathered and blew furiously amongst them. The Canidae cowered in terror.

"You have not behaved like true Humanalia," the Spirit roared, "therefore you will not be infused with the spirit of the wolf. You have decided to show contempt for our sacred ways, making noise instead of keeping silence. The wolf is a creature of honour, it knows how to stay quiet when it is necessary. Therefore YOU will become mere dogs, Simples. This way you can sit about and howl and bark all day long!"

As the Spirit spoke, the Canidae clan began to shrink. They got smaller and smaller. Fur began to cover their bodies and they fell on all fours. Tails sprouted out behind them and when they tried to say sorry and beg for forgiveness, they could only whine.

Realising their loss, they looked at the other clans with eyes full of yearning and longing.

And so it was, that this tribe turned into the first Simples in the Kingdom of Cush.

SIX

PAPA ANANSI AND
MR TURTLE

One day, Papa Anansi went to his garden and picked some very fat, very tasty yams.

He peeled off their rough skin and washed off their pale flesh and baked them with so much care, that they came out smelling delicious. Papa Anansi's stomach began to growl. He could not wait to sit down and eat.

Just then there was a knock at his door. It was Mr Cooter. He had been traveling all day and all night and he was very tired and hungry. The shell on his back felt heavy and he was eager to rest.

"Ah! Hello Papa Anansi," said Mr Cooter.

"I have been walking all day and all night. I passed your house and smelt the most delicious smell. What are you cooking? Is that yams? Please, will you share your meal with me?"

Papa Anansi began to grumble, he could not say no. It was the custom in Cush to share your meal with visitors at mealtime. But Papa Anansi was not happy. He was very greedy and wanted all the yams to himself. He had to think of a plan quickly. "Of course Mr Cooter, please come in. I would be honoured to have you as my guest. Sit down here and help yourself." Mr Cooter crawled slowly inside and sat down, but just as he reached for a yam, Papa Anansi yelled, "*Hei!* Mr Cooter! Do you not have manners? You know better than to come to a table with such dirty hands."

Mr Cooter looked down at his hands. The spider-man was right, they were indeed filthy. He had been crawling all day and all night, and had not had a chance to clean up.

Mr Cooter got up and went to the river to clean his hands. He trudged all the way back up to the house and saw that Papa Anansi had already begun to eat.

"I hope you do not mind, I did not want these tasty yams to get cold, so I started without you," said Papa Anansi, "but now you are back, so join me now."

Mr Cooter sat down and again reached for another yam, but Papa Anansi began to yell at him. "*Hei*! Mr Cooter, did you not hear me before? It is not polite to come to the table with dirty hands!"

Mr Cooter looked down and saw that his clean hands were in fact dirty once more. He had had to crawl on them to get back to the house. So off he went and walked down to the river to wash himself for a second time. When he walked back this time, he was careful to walk on the grass so his hands would stay clean. But by the time he sat down at the table, all the yams were gone! Papa Anansi had finished up every bite and not so much as a morsel was left.

Mr Cooter glared at Anansi. Getting up from the table he said, "thank you for sharing your meal with me Papa Anansi. If you ever find yourself near my house, I would like to return the favour." Then with a small smile, he walked slowly out the door and continued on his way.

A few days later, Papa Anansi saw that his cupboards were bare. There was nothing in his house to eat.

"Oh dear-dear what am I going to do?" he muttered to himself. Then he remembered the meal that Mr Cooter had offered. Excited, he set off to find Mr Cooter's house and was pleased to see the turtle a short while later sunbathing on the riverbank.

"Ah! Hello Mr Cooter! What a coincidence

that I should bump into you today."

Mr Cooter looked up. "Hello Papa Anansi, have you come to share a meal with me?"

"A meal? Oh yes, yes, I forgot about that!" said Papa Anansi his stomach rumbling.

"Great, just give me a moment to prepare." Mr Cooter dove into the river to his underwater house and began to set up the dinner table for two. A few moments later he returned to the bank. "I have made all your favourite foods Papa Anansi and the table is ready to seat you. Please, jump in and join me." Mr Cooter dived back underwater and began to slowly eat his meal.

With a huge leap, Papa Anansi jumped into the river, but he could not reach the riverbed. He tried to swim down, but he was so light that he kept popping back up to the surface. He tried swan dives and belly flops and canon balls. He tried standing on a rock and then jumping into the water backwards, but nothing worked.

While Papa Anansi was huffing and puffing on the bank, Mr Cooter continued to slowly eat.

Papa Anansi was so hungry now, there was no way he was going to give up a free meal. He sat down for a moment and began to plot and think and plan and scheme. Finally he had an idea!

Papa Anansi began grabbing as many stones and rocks as he could and stuffed them into his jacket pockets. This time, when he jumped into the water, he sank right down to the bottom and went to join Mr Cooter.

When Papa Anansi saw the table, his eyes almost popped out of his head. It was full of food! There was yams and plantain and spicy grilled tilapia and bowls of *fufu* and soup. There was *jollof rice* and *gari* and a plate full of *chin-chin.* Papa Anansi's mouth began to water. He couldn't believe how much there was. He could eat his full here, and not have to worry about eating again for the rest of the day. But just as he reached for his first bite, Mr Cooter stopped him. "*Hei!* Papa Anansi! Do you not have manners? You know better than to come to a table with your jacket on!"

Papa Anansi paused. Mr Cooter was right, in Cush it was not good manners to eat with your outside clothes on. He noticed that Mr Cooter had removed his own before sitting down. Papa Anansi began to shrug off his jacket, but the moment it was off his shoulders, he went zooming back up to the surface of the river and popped out onto the riverbank.

Dismayed and still very hungry, Papa Anansi stuck his head down into the water. There was Mr Cooter, still slowly enjoying his wonderful banquet.

The moral of the story? When you try to outsmart someone, you may soon find yourself outsmarted.

SEVEN

PAPA ANANSI AND THE CROCODILE

(Inspired by Indian folklore)

Deep in the jungles of Cush, at the top of a very tall tree that stood by a riverbank, Papa Anansi liked to rest after he had eaten his lunch.

Below him in the river, lived Mrs Nile the crocodile and all her crocodile children.

Everyday Mrs Nile would watch Papa Anansi, round and full and fat, spin his hammock and then lie inside it, snoozing beneath the sun.

"Son," said Mrs Nile one day, "go across the

river and bring that juicy fat Papa Anansi for me, I want to eat him for dinner."

"How can I capture Papa Anansi?" the son exclaimed, "he is the trickiest trickster in the whole Kingdom! Besides, I cannot climb trees and he never comes into the water."

"Think hard my son, I know you will find a way," replied his mother.

After a long time, the young crocodile had an idea. Papa Anansi was known for his fondness of the ripe fruit that grew on an island on the other side of the river, but he could not reach it.

Mrs Nile's son swam to the riverbank and called him down.

"Papa Anansi, Papa Anansi!"

Anansi slowly opened one eye. "What is it?" the spider-man replied, annoyed that his nap had been interrupted.

"I am going to the other side of the island, where the fruit is the sweetest and ripest in all of Cush. Would you like to come?"

"Stupid Reptilia!" spat Papa Anansi, "you know I cannot swim."

"That's alright, I can take you on my back."

Papa Anansi was so greedy, that although he was already full, he still wanted to eat the fruit from the island. So he jumped down from his tree and climbed onto the crocodile's back.

They began to move through the water.

Papa Anansi licked his lips and laughed for joy as he held onto the crocodile's scaly back. Then suddenly, the young croc began to dive.

"Oh no! Help! Someone help me!" Papa Anansi cried. The water began to rise over his head and he was very afraid. He held onto the crocodile tighter and tried to hold his breath.

When they finally rose back up, Papa Anansi began to cough and splutter. "Why did you do that to me? You know I cannot swim!"

"I know, I was trying to drown you," sneered the crocodile. "My mother said you are fat and round and juicy and she would like to eat you."

Papa Anansi thought quickly. "Ohhhh is that it? If only you had told me! I left the tastiest part of myself up in my tree."

"What do you mean?" snapped the crocodile, "I can see how fat and tasty you are right now."

"Yes, but the fattiest, tastiest part of me is my heart and I left that up in the tree."

The young croc thought about this. He knew his mother would be very cross if he didn't bring the *whole* of the spider man.

"Alright," he replied, "we will go back to the riverbank to get it."

And so the silly crocodile turned around and swam back the way they had just come.

The moment they reached the shore of the riverbank, Papa Anansi scuttled back up into his tree.

"Ho!Ho!" he called down to the crocodile in the water, "I am up in my tree with my heart, but if you want it, you will have to climb up and get it!"

Realising he had been tricked, the embarrassed crocodile swam away to find his mother and tell her once again, that Papa Anansi was indeed the trickiest trickster in all of the Kingdom.

EIGHT

PAPA ANANSI AND THE WITCH

One day Papa Anansi's village was hit by famine and drought. All the villagers had to figure out how to survive, including the crafty little spider-man.

In the same village was a witch named "Five". She hated this name and so cast a spell over it so that if anyone used *"Five"*, they would fall asleep for a year.

"Ah-ha!" said Papa Anansi, "I will trick someone into saying the witch's name, then I will go to their house and take even the little food they have and add it to mine, that way I will have enough food to see out this drought."

In his cupboard, the spider-man had saved a little bit of corn. He took them out to the front of his house, separated them into five piles and then sat on one.

Just then Mrs Buttering hopped by. "Hello Mrs. Buttering! Would you like some corn for your children?" he called out.

"Ah! Papa Anansi, you are a good man," replied Mrs Buttering running over.

"No problem, however first you have to tell me how many piles of corn I have and then I will give you one of them."

Mrs Buttering knew the crafty spider man was a tricky little trickster, so she took her time counting the piles. "One...Two...Three... Four...Five!" she cried. The moment she said the witches' name, she dropped to the ground and fell into a deep sleep.

In an instant, Papa Anansi jumped off his corn. He ran to Mrs Buttering's home and took all the food she had been keeping away for her family. The food lasted Papa Anansi for a week before it ran out. After that, he decided he would try his trick again.

Taking his corn out to the front of his house, he separated them into five piles and then sat on one.

Soon Mr Naw-Naw, the squirrel came scampering down the road.

"Hello Mr Naw-Naw. Would you like some corn for your children?"

"Ah! Papa Anansi, you are a good man," replied Mr Naw-Naw running over.

"No problem, however first you have to tell me how many piles of corn I have and then I will give you one of them."

Mr Naw-Naw knew the crafty spider man was a tricky little trickster, so he took his time counting the piles. "One...Two...Three... Four...Five!" he cried. The moment he said the witches' name he dropped to the ground and fell into a deep sleep.

In an instant, Papa Anansi jumped off his corn. He ran to Mr Naw-Naw's house and took all the food he had been keeping away for his family. The food lasted Papa Anansi for a week before it ran out. And so he decided to try his trick again.

Taking his corn out to the front of his house, he separated them into five piles and then sat on one.

Soon Miss Grey the goose came sailing down the road.

"Hello Miss Grey. Would you like some corn for your children?"

"Ah! Papa Anansi, you are a good man," replied Miss Grey running over.

"No problem, however first you have to tell me how many piles of corn I have and then I will give you one of them."

Now Miss Grey knew the crafty spider man was a tricky little trickster, so she took her time counting the piles.

" One...Two...Three...Four and the one you are sitting on!" she cried.

Papa Anansi frowned. "No, no, Miss Grey. If you want some corn, you will have to do it properly!"

And so Miss Grey smiled a small smile and began to count again, "One...Two...Three... Four and the one you are sitting on!"
"NO! NO!" yelled Papa Anansi, angry now, "that is not the way to count! Do it right!"

Miss Grey smiled her small little smile and counted again. "One...Two...Three...Four and the one you are sitting on!"

Papa Anansi became so furious, he jumped down from his pile and decided to show the stupid goose how to count the right way. "That's not the way to count!! You are supposed to say *one-two-three-four-five*!"

As soon as he said the witch's name Papa Anansi dropped to the ground and fell into a deep sleep.

Smiling her small smile, Miss Grey picked up the five piles of corn and took them all home to give to her children to eat.

NINE

FOOLISH BENJAMIN BUTTERING

(Inspired by Indian folklore)

In the Kingdom of Cush, a long time ago, Benjamin Buttering was taking a nap. He began to have a very bad dream.

Suddenly he woke up and said to himself, "what would happen to me if the sky was to fall?"

As he dwelled on this and sat scratching his head, Papa Anansi accidently dropped a coconut from the coconut tree he was sitting in. It fell to the ground with a crash behind Benjamin.

Startled, Benjamin jumped and cried, "oh no, oh no! The sky is falling! The sky is falling!" and he sprang to his feet and ran as fast as his rabbit legs would take him.

He ran past his wife Mrs Buttering who called out, "husband, why are you running so fast?"

"Haven't you heard," said Benjamin, "the sky is falling!"

Terrified, Mrs Buttering joined him. They ran through their clan land and when the other Leporidae heard what was happening, they began running too. Soon there was hundreds of them running through the Kingdom of Cush.

They passed by Doju Deer and told him too, "Doju, the sky is falling! The sky is falling!"

Doju joined them and began running too.

Soon they came to Slothden where all the Ursidae lived, and they told the bears the same thing, "the sky is falling! The sky is falling!"

They ran through the Clouder Land with the prowls and prides of the Pantherinae, and even through the herds of the Elephantidae.

After a while they passed by the palace where King Musa was. He heard the stampede of the clans and their terrified cries.

He found his royal horn and blew into it loudly. When the animals heard this they stopped running.

"What is going on! Why are you all running?" King Musa demanded.

"The sky is falling!" all the Humanalia cried.

"Who told you that? Did you see this happening?" asked King Musa.

"Well, the Pantherinae told us," said the Elephantidae.

"And it was the Ursidae who told us," said the Pantherinae.

"Doju the deer told us your majesty!" cried

the Ursidae.

"It was Mrs Buttering who told me!" said Doju.

"Your majesty, I saw my husband Benjamin running and when I asked him, he told me the sky was falling!" sniffled Mrs Buttering.

"Benjamin," called King Musa, "how do you know the sky is falling."

"I heard it your majesty!" said Benjamin. "I heard a terrible noise after I woke up from my nap and I knew the sky was coming down."

"Very well," said King Musa, "show me the place where you heard this terrible noise."

So Benjamin jumped onto King Musa's back and led him to the spot beneath the coconut tree where he had been sleeping.

When they arrived there, King Musa looked down at the ground and saw the broken coconut.

"This must be what you heard, this coconut fell from the tree while you were asleep."

Just then, Papa Anansi poked his head out from the branches to see what all the fuss was about.

"Papa Anansi, did you drop this coconut from the tree?" asked the King.

"Hmm, yes your majesty. I must have knocked it loose when I was spinning my hammock."

"Benjamin heard the noise and thought the sky was falling."

"Huh!" chuckled the spider man, "Leporidae have never been very bright."

King Musa returned to his palace to tell all the clans that the sky was *not* falling down.

Can you imagine, if the wise and noble King had not stopped them, then all those poor Humanalia would still be running today. All except Papa Anansi of course, he was far too clever for that.

TEN

THE ISLAND OF DEMONS

(Inspired by Japanese folklore)

Long long ago, in the Kingdom of Cush lived an Ursidae called Mr Bear and his wife Mrs Bear. They were poor, but they were hardworking and because of this, they were happy. They were happy for the simple roof over their heads and they were happy for the simple bowl of food they had each day.

However, there was one thing they wanted more than anything, and this made them very very sad. They had never had a child. More than anything they wanted a little boy.

One day Mr Bear went out to the forest to cut down some trees. His wife went down to the river to wash some clothes. As she worked, Mrs Bear began to hum a tune giving praise to Nyame the sky-god and she smiled at the beauty of the flowing water and the green green grass that surrounded her.

Suddenly, she saw something floating down the river towards her. As it drew nearer, Mrs Bear could see that it was an enormous mango, the biggest mango she had ever seen! She grabbed one of her clothes and making a lasso, threw it out to catch the mango. Using all her strength, she drew it to the bank and then picked it up and hurried home.

"Look! Look at what I have found Mr Bear!" she cried as she rushed through the door.

Mr Bear's eyes grew wide with surprise. "My goodness Mrs Bear, what a remarkable piece of fruit. I have never seen anything like it! Where did you buy it?"

"I did not buy it Mr Bear," said his

wife grinning. "I was down by the riverside washing clothes and singing songs of praise to Nyame the sky-god, when this began to float down the stream straight to me!"

"Extraordinary!" said Mr Bear. "This is certainly a gift from heaven and I am sure, will taste delicious." Taking his axe, Mr Bear was about to chop the mango in half when it fell apart. The old couple jumped back in amazement. Inside the fruit, right in the centre where the stone should have been, was a beautiful little cub. He began to gurgle and held his chubby arms out.

"A baby! A baby boy!" cried Mrs Bear. She scooped the cub up and hugged him. "Nyame has certainly given him to us!"

The couple named the child Navajo and brought him up as their own. They lived happily together beneath their simple roof and enjoyed their simple bowl of food. And with a delicious piece of mango to nibble on everyday, the couple were never sad again.

As the years went on Navajo grew big and strong. When he was thirteen years old he went to his parents.

"Father, Mother, all these years you have loved me and taken care of me. Now the time has come for me to take care of you. I am going to go away for a little while but when I come back, I will bring you so many riches. You will never have to worry about anything again!"

"Where are you going to go my son?" asked Mother Bear.

"I am going to the other side of the Kingdom, up in the mountains, where the King has banished the tribe of demons. They are rich but that does not stop them from going into the other clan lands and stealing and killing them. I am going to conquer them and punish them and I will bring some of their wealth to you."

Father Bear lowered his head in dismay. "These demons are terrible creatures my son! They have blood red skin and horns on their heads and terrible teeth and deadly claws. How will you be able to conquer them? You are just a child!"

Navajo replied, "do not forget father, that I am no *ordinary* child. I was sent by Nyame the sky-god and was put in the belly of a mango to come here to you. I can do things no other child can do!"

Both Mother Bear and Father Bear knew this was true, so they packed him some golden fried dumplings for his journey and agreed to let him go.

Navajo was a quarter of the way to the land of the demons, when a Canidae came running up to him.

"*Woof! Woof!* Do you have anything to eat," whined the pup. "I am starving!"

"Yes, of course," replied Navajo and gave

him one of the dumplings. After this the Canidae followed happily after him.

Navajo was halfway to the land of the demons, when a Hominidae came scuttling down the tree and ran up to him.

"H*oo-hooo-hee-ha-ha!* Do you have anything to eat?" chattered the infant. "I am starving!"

"Yes, of course," replied Navajo and gave him one of the dumplings. After this the Hominidae followed happily after him.

Navajo was about three quarters of the way to the land of the demons, when an Arachnida scuttled into his path.

"Ahh! Young Ursidae cub. My name is Papa Anansi. Do you have anything to eat? I am starving," he pleaded.

"Hello Papa Anansi. Yes, of course," Navajo replied and gave the spider-man one of the dumplings. After this Papa Anansi followed happily after him.

Finally, Navajo and his companions came to a river. "Hmm, we have to cross this river so we can get to the land of demons," he told them. Navajo searched around him. He asked his companions to gather all the bits of wood they could find and then he built a boat. Together, they all climbed onto it and drifted across the river.

Suddenly a thick white fog blew around them. It drifted around the boat like a big cloud.

Ahead of them, rising up out of the fog was a fort and sitting in the middle of it was a castle.

Rowing the boat to shore, Navajo and his companions stepped onto the land, and began to make their way towards the castle.

Navajo tried to climb the fort but it was too high.

"Papa Anansi" Navajo said, "climb over this wall and see if there are any demons on the other side." So Papa Anansi spun a web and used it to climb up and over the wall.

A little while later he came back. "Ursidae cub, the demons are all in the castle. Ohhh! What terrible creatures they are. They saw me and tried to stamp on me with their big hairy feet and they chased me away with their clubs and sticks."

"Hmm," replied Navajo. "Hominidae, climb over the wall and unlock that gate over there." So the Hominidae scampered up and over the wall.

A little while later, there was a grating sound and when Navajo pushed the gate, it swung open. He quickly marched inside, the Canidae following behind him. Navajo put his hands to his mouth and called out loudly, "Demons! Demons! Navajo is here to put an end to you."

Hearing the young cub's yells, the demons came rushing out of their castle. They were truly as horrible as Father Bear had said! They had blood red skin and huge mouths with sharp teeth. They had pointed horns that stuck out from their heads and razor sharp claws, and their massive feet were covered with thick green hair.

"Stupid cub," roared the leader of the demons. "First you sent that spindly spider-man and now you dare to summon us. We are going to eat you up and your friends too!"

But Navajo had a plan. "Attack!" he cried.

The Canidae dashed between the legs of the demons biting and snapping at their feet.

Clever Papa Anansi spun some more webs, and the Hominidae used them to swing from demon to demon, punching and choking them with his heavy hands.

The attack was too much for the unprepared demons. "Ouch! Ouch! Stop! Please!" they cried hopping up and down.

Navajo rushed forward and grabbed the

chief demon. "Do you give up?" he cried pulling out his spear and holding it to the demon's throat.

The chief demon tried to struggle and squirm free, but the Ursidae cub was too strong.

"Do you give up!" Navajo yelled again.

"Yes! Yes! Please, make them stop!" begged the chief demon.

Papa Anansi, knowing that the demon's power was in their eyes, spun a poisonous web over their faces, that would blind them forever.

Soon all the demons were standing by, quiet and humiliated. They no longer had the power to attack any of the other clans, and they would never rob or kill again.

"Bring me all your treasures," ordered Navajo. The demons ran back into their castle and returned with gold, silver, jewels and rolls of silk.

And so Navajo, brought the riches back to his father and mother. How pleased the old couple were to see their son again!

As promised, they would never have to worry about food or anything anymore and they all lived happily ever after.

ELEVEN

PAPA ANANSI AND THE GOD OF THE SEA

There had been a long and dry famine in the Kingdom of Cush.

Papa Anansi, who loved to eat, was unable to find any food.

One day he travelled down to the coast and looked desperately out to sea.

Rising out from the midst of the water, he saw a tiny island with a tall coconut tree planted right in its centre. Leaping to his feet, the spider man began to clap and sing with glee. He loved coconuts and if he could reach the tree, then he could get enough coconut water to drink and coconut flesh to eat for months! But how was he going to get to it? Arachnida like him were not very strong swimmers and the sea was very temperamental, she could become furious in the click of a finger.

Papa Anansi looked around the beach. A few feet away he saw what looked like a broken old boat. It did not look strong, but he was a little man and was not very heavy, so he would give it a try. After his first five attempts, it did not go very well. The sea decided to play tricks with him, so every time he got a little nearer to the island, she would send a huge wave and toss him back onto the beach.

However, the little spider-man was not going to give up. On his seventh attempt, the sea now tired of this game, steered him towards the island with the coconut tree on it.

Papa Anansi tied his boat to the trunk of the tree and then scurried up it to its highest branches and began to pluck the rich brown round coconuts. "One – two – three – four," he said dropping them towards his boat. But to his dismay, the coconuts missed the boat each time and fell into the sea, until there was only one coconut left. Papa Anansi took his time and aimed this one as carefully as he could, but he still missed and watched broken hearted as the precious fruit sunk down, down, down towards the seabed.

His stomach growled angrily. He had not even had the chance to taste one and now all the coconuts were gone.

Papa Anansi could not bear the thought of going home empty-handed. He took a deep breath and in his despair, threw himself from the top of the tree into the sea. However, to his complete astonishment, instead of drowning, the little spider-man found himself standing on the seabed in front of a great palace. Out came a merman, with a brass coloured tail and a long white beard.

"Papa Anansi, what are you doing here in Atlantis? What did you want so badly that you came to Poseidon's palace to seek it?"

Anansi told Poseidon his sad story. Touched, the sea-god decided to show the pathetic little land creature some sympathy.

He held up his trident and summoned a cooking pot. He handed the pot over to Anansi. "Here, take this. With this pot, you will never go hungry again. It will always refill itself and supply you with enough food for you and all your friends. All you have to do is tap it on its side three times and say "*pot, pot, do for me what you did for your previous master.*"

Papa Anansi was so grateful, he took the pot from the sea-god and left him with many, many thanks.

Curious to see if Poseidon had been telling

the truth, Anansi decided to test the pot as soon as he climbed back into his boat. He tapped it on its side and said, *"pot, pot, do for me what you did for your previous master."*

Immediately the pot began to fill itself with Anansi's favourite vegetable soup. The spider-man ate until he was good and full.

When he returned to his village, his first thought was to call all the villagers and have a great feast, but Anansi was a greedy man and his selfishness stopped him in his tracks. "What if I do that and end up using all the magic in the pot?" he thought to himself. "Then I would have nothing left!" So instead, he decided to hide the pot and keep it a secret.

The next day, Papa Anansi decided to take a walk, but he had to be careful. He couldn't walk around as if he had energy, he had to look as tired and hungry as everyone else.

"Ah! Mr Dudu, what a terrible famine this is," he said when he passed the weary mole.

Mr Dudu drained by hunger, could merely nod his head. He was surprised that the spider-man even had the strength to talk.

Again, the following day, after eating to his heart's content, Papa Anansi decided to take a walk.

"Ah! Miss Grey, what a terrible famine this is," he said when he passed the weary goose. But Miss Grey, drained by hunger could only nod her head. She was surprised that the spider-man even had the strength to talk and she couldn't be sure, but she thought she heard him burp.

On the third day, the same thing happened. Papa Anansi ate from his pot and then decided to go for a walk.

"Ah! Mr Buttering, what a terrible famine this is," he said when he passed the weary rabbit. But Benjamin Buttering, drained by hunger, could only nod his head. However, his eye did pass over the spider-man for a second and he was certain Papa Anansi looked plumper.

He took his concern to the other villagers.

"Yes! I have been wondering the same thing," hissed Mr Mamba.

"But where is that tricky little trickster getting food! The earth is parched, nothing is growing, there is no food anywhere!" cried Miss Doju.

"I have an idea," said Madame Aedes the mosquito," I will fly into his house and wait in a dark corner of his ceiling. Whatever it is Papa Anansi is doing, we shall soon find out!"

So Madame Aedes, waited in the corner of Papa Anansi's room. Luckily she didn't have to wait long. Back from his recent walk, Papa Anansi returned home feeling hungry. He shut his door and then closed all his windows and then went to take out his pot.

He tapped against its side and sang "*pot, pot, do for me what you did for your previous master."*

Instantly the pot began to overflow with food. Papa Anansi ate heartily and then put it back in its hiding place. Drowsy from his meal, he went to bed and was soon fast asleep.

As soon as he was out, Madame Aedes beckoned to Mr Buttering who was waiting outside. Together they carried the pot to the rest of the villagers.

"Pot, pot, do for me what you did for your previous master," said Madame Aedes and she tapped the pot against its side.

All the villagers looked on in amazement. They ate from the pot and ate from the pot until they could barely move, but then soon something began to go terribly wrong. Because it was producing so much food, the pot grew hot and began to melt.

"Oh dear-dear!" cried Benjamin Buttering, "what are we going to do? Papa Anansi is going to be furious!"

"Quickly, lets replace this pot with another one, that way he will think he has broken it," suggested Mr Mamba.

So Benjamin and Madame Aedes put a new pot in the hiding place of the old one.

Papa Anansi woke up, ready for another meal. He brought out his pot and tapped it on its side *"pot, pot, do for me what you did for your previous master."*

Nothing happened.

He tried again, except this time he spoke more loudly, *"pot, pot, do for me what you did for your previous master."*

Still the pot remained empty. "Hmm, I must have used it too much," Papa Anansi muttered to himself. "As soon as the sun comes up, I will head off towards the shore, get back into my boat and return to the island with the coconut tree."

So the following morning, he did just that.

As soon as he arrived at the island, he did

exactly what he had done the first time. Papa Anansi tied up his boat and then scurried to the top of the coconut tree. This time however, when he threw the coconuts down, they fell straight into the boat. Not one, fell into the sea.

Frustrated, he began to throw the coconuts deliberately into the water and then jumped in after them.

Like the first time, he found himself outside Poseidon's palace, with the sea-god waiting to hear his tale. The merman showed him the same sympathy he had done before and holding out his trident, conjured up a big stick.

Hopping up and down with excitement, Anansi did not wait to hear the full instructions. He swam back up to the surface, got into the boat and tried to see what magic the stick held. *"Stick, stick, do for me what you did for your previous master."*

On command, the stick began to beat him.

"*Hei! Ouch! Ouch!*" cried Papa Anansi. But the stick ignored him and continued to beat him so severely, that he had to jump back into the water and leave the stick and boat behind. Anansi began his sorrowful trip back home covered in bruises.

When he got back, the villagers all came out to see what had happened to him.

"Poor Papa Anansi," hissed Mr Mamba. A loud burp erupted from his lips.

"Yes, poor, poor spider-man," sympathised Miss Grey.

Papa Anansi looked at them. He couldn't be sure, but they all looked plumper and happier than they had the day before....

TWELVE

WHY THE LIZARD
NODS ITS HEAD

(Inspired by West African folklore)

I n the Kingdom of Cush, not far from Papa Anansi's village, there lived a great king. His name was King Musa. The king had three beautiful daughters, but nobody knew their names except for their mother and father.

When the girls were old enough, their father decided that it was time for them to get married and so he made a proclamation:

"Anyone who can tell me the name of my daughters, may choose the one he loves and take her hand in marriage!"

The exciting announcement went all around the Kingdom. When he heard it, Papa Anansi decided that he would like to marry the oldest daughter, as to him, she was the most beautiful of the three. But he had to come up with a clever plan. So he plotted and he thought and he planned and he schemed.

"Ah ha! I've got it!" he cried.

First Papa Anansi bought a large jar of honey. He set off for the hidden lake by the palace, where the King's daughters liked to bathe. When he got there, he climbed to the top of a nearby tree where some delicious fruit grew. He picked some of the fruit, poured honey over it and then waited for the princesses to appear.

Just as the sun rose to its highest point, the princesses approached the lake, ready to bathe. When he saw them, Papa Anansi dropped the fruit from his place in the branches. *Doof!* came the sound, as it hit the ground.

Hearing this, the princesses thought the fruit had dropped on its own because it was ripe. The youngest of the girls ran over and picked it up. When she put it to her lips, the sweet sweet honey made her swoon.

"Oooo! Iyanna, sister, come and taste this fruit!" she exclaimed.

Papa Anansi, from his place in the tree, dropped another piece of fruit.

This time the middle sister heard it and ran over to pick it up.

"Ooo, Masma, this one is even sweeter than the one you just had. Quick come here Mamere, you have to taste it too!"

Clapping his hands with glee, Papa Anansi discovered the names of King Musa's daughters.

As soon as the princesses had gone, he scuttled back down the tree and ran back to his village. He called all the elders and summoned them to a meeting in the King's palace the very next day. Then, he visited his friend Mr Chukwu the Lizard, who was to act as a crier during the meeting in the palace and sound the names of the princesses through his trumpet.

"Ah! But Papa Anansi, you have not told me the names of the girls. How am I to herald them through my trumpet?"

"Hmmm, you are right," replied Papa Anansi. "I will tell you, but you must promise not to tell anyone else." So Anansi revealed to Mr Chukwu, the names of King Musa's daughters.

Early the next morning, the King and all the elders met in his court. Papa Anansi greeted them respectfully, as was custom in Cush, and then began to state his business.

"King Musa, you made a proclamation to the entire Kingdom, that anybody who could tell you the names of your three beautiful daughters, could take the hand of the one he loved in marriage."

King Musa nodded, but inside he was laughing to himself. There was no way this spindly little spider-man had been able to complete such a task.

"Well, I tell you now in front of all the elders that I have done it!"

The King held back a chuckle. "Indeed Papa Anansi, you are known throughout Cush as one of the cleverest amongst all Humanalia. Please tell me now, what is the name of my daughters?"

With a flourish Papa Anansi gestured Mr Chukwu forward. "My dear Mr Chukwu, with your trumpet, please declare the name of the King's youngest daughter."

Mr Chukwu held his trumpet to his lips and played very loudly, "the name of the King's youngest daughter is Masma!"

The King and the elders gasped.

"Now Mr Chukwu, with your trumpet, please declare the name of the King's middle daughter."

Mr Chukwu held his trumpet to his lips and played very loudly, "the name of the King's middle daughter is Iyanna!"

The King and the elders gasped.

"And finally, my dear Mr Chukwu, with your trumpet, please declare the name of the King's oldest daughter."

Mr Chukwu held his trumpet to his lips and played very loudly, "the name of the King's oldest daughter is Mamere!"

King Musa leapt from his throne.

"And she is the one I would like to marry your majesty, because to me, she is the most beautiful," said Papa Anansi.

King Musa placed his head in his hands. He could not go back on his word. He had to fulfil the proclamation as he had declared it.

"Elders, Papa Anansi, Mr Chukwu and to

all those gathered, as promised I will give my daughters to the person who has named them. Therefore Mr Chukwu, I declare that person to be you."

"What!" cried Papa Anansi hopping up and down. "King Musa, it was I, Papa Kwaku Anansi, who found out the name of the princesses. I only told them to this lizard so he could declare them on the trumpet for me! I should at least get to marry Mamere and Mr Chukwu can take his pick of one of the other two?"

But King Musa refused. Papa Anansi stomped back home to the village in a very bad temper and promised himself he would get Mr Chukwu back for stealing his wife. He thought and he planned and he schemed and he plotted. He could not think of a way to *punish* Mr Chukwu, but he had thought of a way to get him back at least.

He returned to the palace and asked King

Musa for help.

"Your majesty," said Papa Anansi, "I am going on a lonnnngggg journey tomorrow. I need to be up at the crack of dawn. To make sure I get to where I am going on time, please your highness, may I borrow that fine cockerel who wakes you up?"

King Musa thought this over. He felt a little bad about what had happened earlier, and so he agreed to lend the spider-man his cockerel.

As soon as night fell, Papa Anansi went back to the palace. He found the sleeping place of the cockerel, seized it and quickly killed it. Then he took the bird to Mr Chukwu's house. He plucked it and cooked it and then placed its feathers under Mr Chukwu's pillow. Then he served up some of the cooked cockerel and put it on a plate near to Mr Chukwu's hand. To make sure, he took some fiery hot peppers from Mr Chukwu's garden and rubbed them on the inside of the sleeping lizard-man's mouth, making him mute.

As the sun rose, Papa Anansi went to King Musa and told him that his bird had not crowed. King Musa was very surprised to hear this, as the cockerel had never done this before. He summoned one of his servants and told them to find and bring the bird to him, but of course, the servant returned empty-handed.

"Perhaps he has been stolen your majesty," suggested the crafty spider-man. King Musa then ordered his servants to search the Kingdom, but there was no trace of him anywhere.

Then Anansi cunningly said, "you know, Mr Chukwu is a bit of a rogue. He showed that yesterday when he stole my wife. I think he is the thief." So King Musa sent his servants to the lizard-man's house.

There, they found the remains of the

cooked cockerel and his feathers under Mr Chukwu's pillow. Poor Mr Chukwu! He was dragged in front of the King and the elders to be questioned, but with his mouth full of pepper, he could not speak and could only move his head helplessly up and down.

King Musa, believing the creature was refusing to speak, judged him of theft. "Mr Chukwu, I am very disappointed in you. Because of your crime, I can no longer allow you to marry any of my daughters. Papa Anansi will now be given this opportunity instead of you."

Papa Anansi was delighted.

Mr Chukwu was put in chains and dragged to the prisons, nodding his head up and down the whole way.

Since then, lizards always move their heads helplessly backward and forward, as if to say "how can anyone be so foolish as to trust that tricky little trickster Papa Anansi?"

THIRTEEN

ANANSI AND THE
WAR GOD KOKOU

(An original story)

The war God Kokou was the fiercest of all the sky-ancestors. He was a fine Equidae, with a silk black coat and strong heavy hooves.

Kokou wielded a magnificent bow and arrow, which was said to be charmed by magic, and during his days walking the earth, he used it to kill the only dragon known to exist. When a Humanalia wanted to invoke bravery and skill in a fight, they would leave him offerings of peanut and banana porridge and roasted fish wrapped in coconut leaves.

Kokou was very fond of these offerings and took great delight in eating them.

One morning, Papa Anansi woke up feeling exceptionally hungry. It had been two days since he had eaten, and his stomach was making angry noises like the growl of a bad tempered Canidae, *grrrrr, grrrr.*

Strolling through his village, he tried to find some food, but it was late and the villagers had already finished their breakfast. Papa Anansi did not think he would make it till lunchtime, his empty stomach demanded to be filled.

Sitting on a rock by the roadside, Papa Anansi began to plot and think and plan and scheme.

After a few minutes, Benjamin Buttering hopped by. He saw the spider-man looking very troubled. The little voice in his head told him to keep walking, because Anansi was well known for his crafty tricks, but his mouth was turned down sadly and Benjamin was too kind hearted to ignore him.

"Dear Papa Anansi, are you alright?" Benjamin asked.

"Oh Benjamin!" exclaimed the spider-man with despair, "what have you done! Why did you upset Mr Dudu?"

"Mr Dudu? I did not upset him, we are the best of friends!" replied Benjamin.

"That is what I told him! But he just went stomping off into that forest. He said he was going to find a big stick to beat you with!"

"Oh dear-dear!" stuttered Benjamin! A big stick? Are you sure?"

"Yes! I tried to stop him but you know how stubborn the Talpidae clan are, especially moles!"

Benjamin scratched the top of his head, right between his big floppy ears. What could he have possibly done?

"I saw Mr Dudu yesterday when I took

three yams from his garden. He did not seem upset then?"

"Did you pay him?" asked Papa Anansi.

"No, we are the best of friends, we share our vegetables all the time!"

"Mmmmhhhmmm," Papa Anansi hummed.

"I will go into the forest," said Benjamin, "when I find him I will explain everything. We can talk this out, I'm sure it is a simple misunderstanding!"

But Papa Anansi jumped up and grabbed Benjamin's arm. "Do you see this bump on my head?" he pointed to a lump he had gotten by taking a nap beneath a coconut tree, "Mr Dudu did this to me when I tried to talk to him!"

Hopping anxiously from shoe to shoe, Benjamin wrung his paws. What was he going to do? He had never been in a fight before and he wasn't sure he could win one, even if Mr Dudu was smaller and slower and had to wear thick glasses to see.

"I have an idea," said Papa Anansi carefully, "why don't you invoke the strength and skill of Kokou? That way you can defend yourself."

"What a brilliant idea!" cried Benjamin. "But I have never done that before, I'm afraid I've forgotten what to do?"

"You have to go back home and make the creamiest most delicious banana and peanut porridge. Then you have to find two of the fattest tastiest fish, grill them and wrap them in coconut leaves. When you are finished, you have to climb the branches of the mighty oak and make your offering."

"But Papa Anansi, I cannot climb trees! How will I make my offering?"

The spider-man became very serious and sighed deeply and loudly. "Hmm, that is a problem. I will tell you what Benjamin, I was just on my way to the market, but because

I am so fond of you, I will help. Bring the offering here and I will climb up to the highest branches of the mighty oak and hand your offering to Kokou myself."

"You would do that for me?" replied Benjamin brimming with gratitude.

"Of course, but you must hurry, Mr Dudu will be back any moment!"

And so off Benjamin skipped to prepare the sky-ancestors meal.

The moment he disappeared, Papa Anansi raced to Mr Dudu's shop. The mole-man was doing what he did every day, repairing old watches and clocks.

"Hello Papa Anansi," he greeted the spider-man.

"Oh Mr Dudu, what have you done?"

"Me?" asked Mr Dudu pushing his huge glasses up his nose, "I haven't done anything?"

"Benjamin Buttering has been hopping

through the village looking for you. He is as angry as a fire ant. He is shouting that he is going to find a big stick and hit you with it!"

"A big stick! Papa Anansi, are you sure? Benjamin is my very best friend. He wouldn't want to hurt me."

"He said those yams you gave him yesterday, were full of worms and made him sick."

"My yams? Full of worms?" said Mr Dudu puzzled, "they are the best yams in all of Cush! Are you certain he said they made him sick?"

Papa Anansi pointed to the lump on his head. "You see this? I got this when I tried to tell him the same thing!"

"Oh dear-dear!" cried Mr Dudu in despair. What was he going to do? He had never been in a fight before and he wasn't sure he would win one, even if Mr Buttering was soft and cuddly and couldn't squash a mosquito.

"I have an idea," said Papa Anansi carefully, "why don't you invoke the strength and skill of Kokou? That way you can defend yourself."

"What a brilliant idea!" cried Mr Dudu. "But I have never done that before, I'm afraid I've forgotten what to do?"

"Go home, make the creamiest most delicious banana and peanut porridge you can. Then, find two of the fattest tastiest fish, grill them and wrap them in coconut leaves. When you are done, climb the branches of the mighty oak and make your offering to Kokou."

"But Papa Anansi, I cannot climb trees! How will I make my offering?"

The spider-man became very serious and sighed deeply and loudly. "Hmm, that is a problem. I'll tell you what Mr Dudu, I was just on my way to the market, but because I am sooooo fond of you, I will help. Bring the offering here and I will climb up to the highest branches of the tree and hand your offering to Kokou myself."

"You would do that for me?" replied Mr Dudu brimming with gratitude.

"Of course, but you must hurry now, Benjamin will be here any moment."

So off Mr Dudu went.

A short while later, Benjamin returned carrying the delicious food in a basket. Papa Anansi's eyes flew open in delight! Grabbing the treat, he quickly ran up the oak tree and settled himself amongst its leaves. When he had finished eating, he wiped his mouth and returned to the ground.

"What did Kokou say?" asked Benjamin excitedly.

"Oh! He was very pleased with you Benjamin. Yours was the best offering he has ever received. He said you should go and find the biggest stick you can, you are now a skilled fighter!"

Pleased with himself, Benjamin puffed out his chest and entered the forest.

A few moments later, Mr Dudu also returned carrying a basket and again Papa Anansi snatched it up and scrambled to the highest branches of the oak tree.

As he finished wiping his mouth, he heard shouts coming from the ground. Cautiously peeping down, he saw a furious Benjamin standing beside an even angrier Mr Dudu. They were both holding very big sticks!

"Papa Anansi come down from that tree!" they cried.

"No!" Papa Anansi shouted back. "First you put down your sticks!"

"You cannot stay up there forever!" warned Mr Dudu.

"Yes I can!"

"You will get hungry and have to come down sooner or later," said Benjamin. "When you do, we will be here waiting for you!"

And so during the day Benjamin stood beneath the tree, then at night it was Mr Dudu.

Poor Papa Anansi! Two days came and went and his stomach began to growl again, *grrrrr, grrrrr.*

Distressed he turned to Kokou. "Help me! Oh help me great sky-ancestor!"

From his place within the clouds, Kokou looked down. He had seen everything that had happened and was very angry with Papa Anansi for eating his offering.

He decided to teach the tricky little trickster a lesson.

"I will help you Anansi, but only if you can answer this riddle, "what belongs to you, but other people use it?"

Papa Anansi scratched his head. Something that belonged to him but other people used it....? Could it be his house? No, he hardly let anyone in his house.

"Anansi, Anansi! Come down right now!" came the cries from below.

Papa Anansi thought harder. Perhaps it was his wheelbarrow? No, he never let anyone use that either.

"Anansi! Anansi! Come down right now!"

The spider-man thought hard and he thought long. He wished Benjamin and Mr Dudu would stop shouting, they were making it difficult for him to concentrate.

"Anansi! Anansi! Come down right now!"

Suddenly Papa Anansi had the answer. "My name! It is my name!" he whooped with glee. "Something that belongs to me but other people use it!"

"Very good," replied Kokou. "From now on whenever anyone has an offering for me, they will cry out your name *'Anansi! Anansi,'* and you will carry it up this tree to give me."

And so from that day forward, Papa Anansi was at the beck and call of the entire

Kingdom. He carried the baskets of banana and peanut porridge and grilled fish wrapped in coconut leaves, up the mighty oak to Kokou for anyone who called out his name. He was not allowed to eat any, not even a little bite and every time he climbed the tree his stomach would go *grrrr, grrrr, grrrr.*

THE STORY
CONTINUES...

ABOUT THE AUTHOR

Georgina Simmons

Georgina Simmons was born in Accra, Ghana in 1979. She came to London with her mother in 1980 to begin her new life in the UK.

As a child, she always had her nose buried in a book, lost in worlds that had seemingly endless possibilities, and characters moulded by creative minds. It was no wonder then, that she started writing stories and poetry as young as age 5.

Georgina credits Toni Morrison as her first great literary hero, specifically the late author's masterpiece 'Bluest Eye'.

"Ms Morrison taught me everything I would come to know about world building, unique language, and how to write boldly and unashamedly."

'The Chronicles of Jozzie Taylor - The Kingdom of Cush' is Georgina's first novel, followed by book two in the series "The Prince of Atlantis."

Her contemporary short story 'The Bird' was published in the 'Ink Academy Anthology- A Collection of New Writing' in October 2017.

In 2018, her flash fiction crime stories; 'The State of Man', and 'My Brother's Keeper', was published in Culture World's anthology, 'Shots in the Dark'.

'The Bird' makes an appearance in Georgina's own collection of short stories titled 'The Tales We Do Not Tell,' which was released in July 2020. The stories are a macabre narrative of human experiences such as love, hate and vengeance, with alarming religious undertones.

BOOKS BY THIS AUTHOR

Honey Bair And Her Fantastically Fabulous Fables

The Chronicles Of Jozzie Taylor - The Kingdom Of Cush

The Chronicles Of Jozzie Taylor - The Prince Of Atlantis